BOOKS BY SHAY

The Line

The Hacker Angel

Prayer to Jesus

Angelic Advice

The Intercessors Autobiography

Bipolar Disorder Manual

The Angel Interviews

The Perfect Author

Copyright © 2016 Shay Villere

All rights reserved.

ISBN-10: 1539775003
ISBN-13: 978-1539775003

The Magic Man

SHAY VILLERE

9am Sacramento - Home:

Black deck, check. Blue deck, check. Got to have one of those. Red deck, check. A white deck because sometimes it can work. Lots of weenies, but if you do it the right way it can really crush black stuff. Okay, check. All of it in my case. Cool. People hate my case, they say it looks like it has a nuclear detonator in it. Hahah!

Okay, gotta check the email real quick. Nothing new. Awesome, and I am off!

The walk between my brother's house and my parent's house is just about three hundred feet. Really convenient. Love living with my brother, but having mom and dad nearby is convenient. After all, who really wants to cook anyway.

Slide on a marvel shirt. Wolverine works. Grab the phone and the wallet, and then I hit the pavement.

It is such a nice day. Damn, gotta love this weather! On a good day Sacramento really feels like San Diego. Not nearly all the attractions and opportunity, but there are worse places to live. The family originally lived in New Orleans, but moved to Sacramento in 1987 when Mom decided she was tired of the city. Too bad, growing up there might have been fun, or so I hear from my old classmates.

As I get up to the intersection between our houses, a four way stop, I spot a white Mercedes driving from the left side, coming near the stop sign. He slows his vehicle for about five seconds, then just tears through the stop sign. Bastard! Why do people do this? I swear, it is always assholes in luxury cars!

Maybe I have seen this too many times. Maybe I am having a bad day. I guess when you have the power to fight dickheads like this you don't have a choice. Oh well. Here we go again!

I flip a switch on my case and drop it to the ground. A spring action holster in the top corner edge of my case opens and launches my .22 into the air. I catch it in my left hand and size up the Mercedes as it continues down the road. This guy drives fast, but not fast enough....

Pop pop! His head explodes all over what must be white leather. Tough day for him!

Doesn't every Magic player stock a little protection? Ever since the Pro Tour in Moscow, I never leave the house without a piece.

"Hey mom!" My mom is the coolest. There is nothing this lady cannot handle.

"Hey sweetie! How is your day?" she chirps, looking up from the knitting she is working on.

"Pretty good. Hey, there is a mess down the street. Would you please have someone deal with that?"

"Josh, damn, what is it about white Mercedes? Ya gotta kill every rich pencil-neck that drives by?" She set down her knitting and grabbed an iPad. A few clicks later and a cleanup team is dispatched.

"Armando does not care. You know he wants me to practice with the .22. Tell him it was on the job training. So what?" I start walking toward the back door.

"Your dad would not be pleased." Mom was back to her knitting.

"And how long has dad been gone?" My tone was not joyous.

"Oh, I don't know Josh. You know those embedded jobs. I think he has been away for a couple months now."

"Why? How much money does he need?" My tone was getting a little harsh, but she knew what I meant. Dad worked a lot, but it seemed he never really got where he wanted to go.

Government assassins were cheaper than freelance, but the glory factor was low and the work was long and hard. He had been scoping the governor of LA for awhile. Maybe he was almost done, maybe not. We would probably never know.

"C'mon Josh. You know it is not the money."

"Whatever. I have a game to get to." With that I walked out the back door and headed for the garage.

10am Sacramento - Adventures In Comics And Games:

I pulled open the door. The place was a massive dump, but it was the only place in town where you could get an EDH game going almost any waking hour. I waved at the toothless guy behind the counter.

"Hey Josh. What is up in your world today?" Anton was a nice guy. Very smart. He loved gaming, but was so sharp he used to teach java for Oracle employees. We played when we could, but usually my job and his job got in the way. I do not think Anton could do what I do. He definitely could not enjoy it as much.

"Whatcha need today, buddy?"

"Just a water for now." I set my case down and surveyed the room. As usual, a group of fatties and nerds. But they played Magic, and that was my goal at the moment. A few games of Magic before the day got rolling. I spotted Lauren, a guy who was always well put together. A Steelers fan, and everyone always knew it from his garb. "What's up bud?"

"Ah, you know Josh. Just the usual. What's up in your land?" He unzipped his backpack and grabbed a deckbox.

"Nothing big. Little trip later today, but I got an hour for a game."

"EDH?"

"Sure, I guess. You know I like sixty card better though."

"Josh, no one else in the store has power ya know."

"Hey man, can I help it if everyone but me is a loser?" I started shuffling my deck, setting my general, Thassa, on my deckbox.

"Where do you get all this money anyway? I swear, you are the most secretive guy here!"

He laughed.

"Can I help it if everyone here works at Taco Bell?" I grabbed a couple six-sided dice and rolled them. An 8. "Well, better than average, right?"

"C'mon Josh, you are just from a rich family."

"How did I get that fucking label? A few beta moxes and suddenly I am some multimillionaire?"

Lauren is a nice guy, but even nice guys can go too far.

"Whatever, let's play."

And the game was on.

11am Sacramento – Sub Depot Down the Street:

"So you wiped a guy in a Mercedes because he drove through a stop sign." Jeff knew me, but yeah, this morning might have taken things too far. "Josh, you know cleaning up messes is not free. Cleaners gotta be paid. Suppliers gotta be paid. I know you don't want to move again."

"No, I do not want to move again, bitch." I gave him a little shit, but part of what he said was right. Moving always did suck, and dusting a jerk because of bad road rage was not the smoothest thing to do. "So where am I going?"

"Just into the city. You'll be back later today." Jeff slid some papers to me.

"Normal thing or something fun?" I looked over the papers and spotted something that jumped at me. A certain face caught my eye. No way! This was ridiculous. It could not be him!

"Something different I guess." Jeff looked past me.

"Uh, Jeff. This is beyond different!" I realized how loud my voice was, but quickly lowered it. I started looking through the papers some more.

"So what's really different. A guy went too far, some people want him killed. No sweat." Jeff always talked with his hands, and it never failed to bother me. He was from NYC, but no one knew why he had moved to Sacramento. I guess the price was right.

"Well, the fee must be high." I slid the papers into my case.

"No. Normal fee." Jeff cracked his knuckles.

"Oh really."

"Yes really, dipshit. You make plenty. The boss says it's a one day job, so you get a one day fee." Jeff slid his chair back, scratching the hell out of the floor and creating a terrible squeal at the same time.

"So where is the backup?" Yeah I was good, but not this good. This assignment was stretching it as far as I could tell. Sure, I could just take a position and line up a rifle, but the target was too high profile. If something went wrong I was screwed.

"No backup. You can handle it big guy. Enjoy the rest of your day. Don't fuck up."

"Well Jeff, if something happens, I guess you'll be the first to know won't you."

"You better believe it sweety." And with that he strolled out the door.

Gavin Newsom. The mayor of San Francisco. A younger guy, but considered to be a contender for the next gubernatorial election. He had been very supportive of the LGBT community, but was that really worth killing over? Well, that was not my deal. He was getting very dead soon, and that was all I cared about.

Dad worked these jobs usually. You know, one branch of government always trying to wipe out the other side. Libs versus Neocons. The argument would go on till the end of time, but how had Newsom been so crucial that the Neocons were sending me. It did not make sense. But I was not in the business to pull the strings. I was in the business to get paid. Stanford did not come cheap.

I picked up my case and stepped outside. It was 90 minutes to the city. 90 minutes back if traffic was kind to me. But I did not travel in luxury. One of the reasons I was one of the most in demand assassins in Sacramento was because I was a ghost usually, when I was not slicing up the brain of a guy in a Mercedes. I took the bus most places, and sometimes even walked. Sure, if someone ever placed my face, I might be in trouble, but that was not my worry. What these guys did not know was that I killed for fun. The money was nice, and that is what I told everybody, but who really wanted to do the bullshit kid stuff. The world was hell as far as I was concerned, and I was there to tear it up some more. Fun, yes. Maybe it did not make sense to your average doughnut store operator, but I liked killing. It felt empowering. Taking someone's life as if it was yours to take. And the guns were fun too! I did not have some huge collection. But what I had worked. It worked well.

I typically used H20 bullets. No remains. The bullet disappeared within minutes of impact. And they were hollow point. Guaranteed explosion inside the target. Usually I was nowhere nearby, but obviously I wanted my marks to die quickly. I was not one of these finesse killers you hear about in

TV and movies. I did one thing, and one thing alone. Remote firepower. When you are nowhere near the scene, nothing gets traced back.

And my guns, well, my guns were the best part. Made from industrial plastics in my own 3D printer. No need to buy anything. I made my own equipment. Remote device planted in the right spot. The equipment incinerated after the job, and was usually so far away it was never found by anyone anyway.

San Francisco was really not that far, but a bus would have been pushing it. Grabbed my hacked phone, stolen at a magic grand prix the weekend before. In a minute I had a luxury Uber SUV waiting for me. Obviously most 16 year old assassins would not have the money for that, but hey, I was special.

10am New Orleans - Parking Lot of the Superdome:

"Where is it John."
"Where is what asshole." This game would not go on much longer. I was losing blood quickly. What was the point of giving up our position if I was gone soon anyway. But did the guy really have to be such a cock. This may have been the third or fourth time I was tortured, but these guys were fucking things up royally. If they killed me soon there was no gain.

"John, I am only gong to ask one more time. And if you feel the need to withhold your son's position, we will find him anyway." He twirled a scalpel in his left hand. In his right was a GLOC 50 caliber. I was well trained to deal with both, but this guy might get me anyway.

"I have no knowledge of my son's position. He could be anywhere in the world at this point. You guys seem to have so much power, but you cannot find one little 16 year old kid? Who works for you, burger servers?" I laughed, and puked up blood at the same time. Yeah, I was fading but whatever. I was doing my job, and this dildo was not going to crack me.

"John, I have grown tired of you. We spend all these months tracking you. Countless time and resources. All to find you in this pit of a city. Working for the US govt of all criminals. The guys you trust to keep your little crusade going. Now you are going to die for a cause that no longer exists."

"Fuck off asshole. I do not care what you think." I sprung up from my chair and lunged at my captor, unclipping my handcuffs as I slid closer to him.

Bang.

I guess Josh is on his own.

11am Vallejo – En Route to San Francisco:

Hey, a guy has to eat. As I finished my double double, the drone landed a few feet away. You have to love drones, they definitely get the job done. No point in carrying my own guns when a drone can do the job more easily and quicker. I walked over and unhooked the package. Then I flipped a little switch on the drone and a timer started ticking down from sixty. I walked back to the Uber SUV and got in the back seat.

"Hey, let's go already. I am on a schedule."

"Sure boss. Whatever you say." Even in Northern Cali the Uber drivers were all brown and 45 years old. I do not discriminate. Whatever gets the job done.

We were about fifty feet away when the drone exploded. Hopefully no injuries...but do I care? Not particularly. I kill people for a living remember. I don't know where my dad is, but he is out killing people too. So on with the mission.

Okay....for this job we are going with the whole blame it on a Muslim terrorist kick. So suicide bomber it will be. A little package slipped into the purse of an audience member and things should be sweet. Few people get scooped in the way...whatever.

Time for a little nappy-poo. That match against Lauren lasted longer than I really wanted. Oh well. Who knew a job was on the way. A man gotta make his money. I kicked back and slipped into a quiet snooze.

11am New Orleans – Seedy Bar:

"He went quietly I hope." Smoke filled the air. New Orleans still loved it's smoking. And if you were in this business you were used to it anyway.

"Here is the package. It was within one of the tires." He set a small metal credit card on the bar.

"Gosh, here we are on the doorstep of World War III and the US is still hiding data in plastic strips. Amazing! Almost like they are too busy to care about their information because the bombs are more important." He coughed and took a swig from his beer. Lots of beer in New Orleans. Ya gotta love a city that eats breathes and sleeps with a bottle at it's mouth.

"So what do we do now?" He looked out the window. "I hate this place. The whole city smells like urine." He straightened his sleeves and arranged his tie.

"Well we have to get his son now. The guy obviously loved backup plans because his goddamn son is a motherfucking killer too." He laughed, fat as fuck as he was. This guy enjoyed his business, but it is not like he had options. Just another chink in the chain that formed international crime. Who knew where he was from, but did it matter? They were all pieces of shit.

"Let's get a nice ride this time."

"With Maurice at the helm? Right. You are lucky he does not ship you in a crate." Swig of the bottle.

"Whatever, give me the info."

"It is in your watch. Get the fuck out of here. If you don't like my city I do not want to be around your faggity ass." The fat guy turned back toward the bar.

"Fuck off chink. At least I can get laid."

"Guys don't count."

And with that he turned toward the door and motioned to the car down the street. It would not take long to get to California, but who enjoyed flying anymore. You do enough hours in the air and eventually it grinds into you, but killers have to make money too. Hence you do a lot of flying.

12pm San Francisco – Street Level Near Downtown:

Let's see, who will work best. I am thinking the older the better. Hopefully with a Muslim hoodie. That would be perfect. Oh.....there she is. Ask and ye shall receive.

I started walking toward her, sliding the device into my wrist sleeve. A crowd had begun forming around the stage. It was set up in one of SF's biggest park areas. Lots of kids running here and there. Not enough parents to watch the kids. This should not be too tough. All these bitches were covered with a goddamn carpet. And who in SF does not have a huge purse to match their huge head gear.

I got up close, tripped, fell into her, and the device was placed. She turned and looked at me for about one point five seconds and then scurried away, kids in hand. No problemo. A quick platitude from my lying lips and she kept walking toward the event.

Gavin was giving a speech on women's rights to be gay. Awesome. Go gays! It will be funny that a bomb from a chick's handbag would close out his political dreams. Who knew, right? Gotta get on with your life somehow, and mine was packing big bucks with a few skills learned from the fam. That makes me think. I need to give dad a call.

I jumped back into the Uber. He was waiting for me at a Starbucks. You know in movies and TV they always say that assassins like to witness the crimes, but we never care! That is just a cliche'. We could not care less. If most of us could make money watching TV, that is what we would do.

Okay, popping open my iPad. Let's see how the speech goes. It was not televised but the company always has a few hacked cameras in any downtown spot. Just a few data points later and I have Gavin's smiling mug on the screen. And off he goes.

12pm Airborne - Somewhere Over NorCal:

"What's the kid's name?" The plane was tech heavy but plush heavy too. There were enough seats for an entourage, but not a military detail. The man speaking was old and grey, but still looked like he could bust some heads. This was Maurice Devereaux, high end power broker and keeper of dark secrets. His face was not on a database. His face was on ALL the databases. He had a million warrants out on him, but somehow he managed to disappear at the right times.

"Josh Boudreaux."

"Boudreaux .....the fuck did he get a name like that?"

"Probably the same place you did old man." He looked out the window.

This trip was a little different than most operations Maurice was involved with. He enjoyed his fine wine and hookers more than work. But what criminal didn't? Unfortunately Maurice was working for a very high level client today, so he managed to scramble a jet and make sure things were done right.

"So where is he?" Cigarette was lit. A topless waitress dropped off a martini on a finely varnished table.

"Aren't all 16 year old assassins in Sacramento?" A hint of a smile crossed his mouth. The waitress motioned to him. "Just a little OJ sweety. No extra milk please."

"Wow, the center of CA govt. Must be lots of work. I hear more battles are waged there than online." Maurice tapped a screen in front of him. "No address though. Wonder how they managed that."

"The kid plays a lot of Magic The Gathering. We have tapped the NorCal Magic page and come up with an alias that is probably him. Should not take too long to get the intel we need to get him."

"Okay, well, enjoy...we're close enough. Have a fun ride." The seat he was sitting on fell through the floor. A few seconds later it was a drone. It would make the trip to Sacramento in the next twenty minutes.

The floor closed back up. Maurice motioned to his stewardess.

"Babe...bj...make it quick. I have work ya know." As the stewardess started working, Maurice made a phone call.

"Yeah, we need help on this. There...uhhh...is more to this kid than most. He's John Boudreaux's son." Blam...Maurice shot his wad. The stewardess wiped her mouth and kissed his cock, then zipped him up. "No shit, I know people are busy. But look, the kid could be trouble, and we don't even have his location yet. The fag in the suit thinks he can track him, but I doubt it will be that easy." The plane began its descent into the Bay Area.

"Hey sugartits...the purple suit. Gotta make an impression on Gavin. He could be governor soon."

1pm Sacramento – Older Brother's House:

"You could have been a little more precise, Josh." My brother always bitched at the worst times.

"Hey, pipe down in the peanut gallery! Did you score 100k this morning?" He shook his head. My brother Shay, so smart, so beautiful, but just a massive buzzkill sometimes.

"Listen...I am getting away from the killing. No reason anymore. I can slice up banana republic govt systems and make the same, without all the blood. How many other folks were in your bombing this morning?" Shay walked over to his Lazy Boy and flipped on the TV.

"Can I help it if it is fun? Dad likes it too ya know." I pulled out a pack of gum and slid one in. "Gavin did bite it, right? I would not want to piss off the client."

"Yeah, Newsom is not so new anymore. Neither is that cloud of Muslim parts. Must have been fun swirling up the hate storm on that one. Do you ALWAYS have to throw the blame on the west? That strategy might be a little overdone by now. All the guys in the East do it too, almost daily. Get creative at some point. Take a lesson from mom." Shay was already into the boob heavy movie of the afternoon.

"Mom uses too many knives. I am not motivated enough to put that much work into it."

"Hey, a lot of loving care went into that work. She and Dad really are birds of a feather. Mom with the knives, Dad with the bow and arrow." He laughed. So did I. We really did think it was funny. Watching them work together felt like a comic book.

"So why Gavin? Who did he piss off? No one cares about the governor's race. In fact, word on the street is that he is...was...not completely set on doing that race. Whoever wanted your guy dead really really wanted him dead. Hell...I could have scandalized his history with just a few keystrokes. You know what I can do with Photoshop." Channel changed, but the boobs did not.

1pm Adventures:

"Geez, you smell like gunpowder and jizz. What the fuck did you do this morning?" Lauren was always asking questions.

"Little trip. Nothing serious. Let's get back to the game."

The shop was pretty busy today. Seemed like the Magic world worked on a second half of the day clock. I guess that made the most sense since most of this guys were disability hogs who worked off of welfare. Sad state of affairs really. Maybe one day I will teach them how to actually work for a living. If you can call what I do work. Just fun in my world. Lots and lots of fun.

Lauren had exploded right off the bat with three creatures on the first turn. A second turn Balance and I was back in the game. Two pro-black white knights later, followed by an Armageddon, and the game was over. Funny how old tech can still wipe out new ideas. As if any of these guys ever thought for themselves. Seems like all of the decks come from online brain-trusts now. Not the way it used to be, or so Shay tells me.

It was the end of a long MTG decompression session. Nothing better to cap off a kill than a little card game. I stood up from my chair and turned toward the door. What I saw was not only surprising, but painful. I had not seen these guys in years. They were players from San Jose, walking into MY HOMESTORE here in Sacto. These guys were the ultimate in ego but usually they could back it up. What got me in the gut was that their DCI rating was higher than mine. Three guys, all as good as any pro, but what I did not know was going to make all of it even more shocking.

The leader of the pack, Gerald, a true asshole by any scope of the imagination, walked up to me while his crew veered toward the singles counter. Only the best cards made the counter, with many of them reaching into the high three figures. May not seem like much but to magic losers it was a real big pricetag.

"What's up big man? Flashing any moxen today?" Gerald asked, a sly smile crossing his lips.

"Not really, just on my way home." As I started to walk by Gerald, a view from outside surprised me. Not so much because of what it was, but because it was here, in a magic shop, and not in some far corner of the planet.

"Oh, that is too bad Josh, I was hoping to get it on. No time for a quick match?" Gerald flashed a twenty dollar bill in my face. People did still play for ante, but not frequently, and these guys were never rich. But no one knew I would sooner set fire to a Jackson rather than bother fighting over it.

"Maybe later man. I have to get going."

"Whatever dude. Leave it to the big ballin Josh Boudreaux to run from a match with twenty dollars on the line." He laughed, but I could not care less. The front door of the shop opened, and who walked in was quite a surprised.

"Been awhile son. What's shaking in your world?"

Dad!

1pm The Buildings Across from Adventures:

"Get this right asshole or I will cut your hands off and do it for you." Tough business. If you cannot cut it stop wasting your time and bus tables or something. I was here for a job, and no other reason. I may be gay but I was not stupid. And the Boudreauxs are rarely together, hence we needed to get this done now or never.

"No problem. I have them lined up. Which one do you want first?"

"Like I care. Blow up the whole damn shop if you have to. Dead is dead. Email me the video later. I am off to deal with the mom. Word is she is quite a piece of work herself."

The rifleman lined up his shot. He started to squeeze the trigger but as the bullet was about to be fired a blade sliced through the air and cut his hand off.

"Motherfucker! Arrrghghgh!!!! What the fuck?" The assassin dropped his gun and went running down the street. The handler looked back from his car just in time to see a foot smash his face in. Who would have guessed. Apparently mom got to them before they got to her.

Things just got interesting.

1pm The Car:

"The hell was that?" Josh was pissed, and understandably so. Almost getting killed unnerves 16 year olds. Even if they are trained assassins.

"There was a contract dropped on you two. Courtesy of someone Dad pissed off probably. What's up with that John? Can't you keep your spooks out of the family's world?"

"Well, you obviously had no trouble dealing with them. What, Shay pick that up somehow? I knew training that kid to hack was a good idea." John smiled. Ah, the glow of a proud dad.

"Listen folks, we have gotten into quite a mess. The govt guy Josh wasted earlier today was into deep shit, and I mean the deepest." Mom was worried, and that was a new mode for her. This should be interesting.

"What? I have killed govt guys before. Usually no flack. And usually no one knows. All the info comes through Jeff and we have been working with him for years. Since I was 12, at least." John smiled. Ah, the proud father.

"Well, listen Josh, Newsom was already lined up to cheat the next gubernatorial race. He had more rigging set up than a fishing fleet. Take a moment and ask yourself what you think would happen if an actual competent governor got to the top of CA state government?"

"Good things?"

"Well, yeah, but not for assassins. It would be like the wild west. Our communication lines would be cut, law enforcement would be competent, there would be transparent taxation reporting. Terrible stuff really."

"Wait a second." John interjected. "California has been corrupt for a long time. One governor could not undue decades of corruption. And Newsom is not capable enough to do any of that anyway."

"He is with help." Mom's face was stern. "The right kind of help."

"No way, not him." John replied. "No way in a million years would he bother with something like this." He looked away, shaking his head.

At that instant a missile hit the road right in front of the Boudreaux's car. The car went flying off the road into a ditch.

2pm Office – Undisclosed Location:

"Yes sir, the Boudreaux's have been exterminated. Like the rats they have become since moving to Sacramento." the voice on the phone said.

"Good. Too bad about the fag, but hey, he was unprepared. Fuck him." smoke wafted from behind a perfectly appointed chair. The chair swiveled back around to face the rest of the office. There was one person sitting in the chair in front of the desk. The lighting of the room shielded his face. He started to speak.

"So the job is done. Newsom is dead?" The voice was unmistakable. Everyone on earth knew this man.

"Yes Mr.President, Newsom is dead." another puff on the cigar from the fat man behind the desk.

"Wow, I always wanted to have someone killed." The man stood, his face revealed.

"Hillary should have no trouble, sir. Money well spent." a wry smile from the fat man.

"Maurice, you have done an excellent job for our country. Today, the Boudreaux's, tomorrow, the white house!" Bill Clinton laughed, and Maurice joined in.

2pm North Korea:

I spit blood as I woke up. The hell was going on.

"John, glad you are awake. It has been an interesting day for your family."

"The fuck do you know about my family." John could barely lift his head.

"Well, frankly, they are dead. No more sons. No more wifey. All dead." A villainous laugh from the smoke filled side of the room. Two guards were in the room carrying massive assault rifles.

"You are dead you know." John was still so tough. No family. Still tough.

"Now John, come on man. You are locked up. You have been tortured for several hours. You have been flown from New Orleans to North Korea faster than any man ever. What makes you think you can get out of my prisons?"

"Kim...you are such a dumb mother fucker." With that John pulled his arms from behind his back and lunged at the North Korean leader.

"Get him!" Kim said, but the guards seemed immobile. John walked up to the leader and snapped his neck.

3pm Sacramento – Roadside Ditch:

"Holy motherfuck......what was that." Josh was surprised, and just a little short of royally pissed.

"That is what they call a satellite guided, drone delivered, antitank missile kid." Mom was not enjoying the day.

"So who would bother doing all that for us?" Shay posed.

"Isn't it always the usual actors guys? Some asshole behind a desk who wants his pile of money to keep growing?" Dad suggested, knocking some dirt off his suit the way secret agents always do after almost dying via missile attack.

"So what do we do now?" Josh asked, making sure all of his hidden guns were still in functional order and ready to use.

"I want to kill somebody." Shay said, looking like quite the pissed assassin-turned-hacker.

"I thought you were deep in hack world, asshole." Josh replied, starting to walk down the street.

"Like this is any better? I do not enjoy missile attacks. Dad might, but not me." Shay said, as Dad smiled.

"Guys, lets stuff the bitching and get moving, obviously we are not safe, as many knives as I might have shoved in strange places." Mom said, and the family started hustling down the street.

3pm Washington DC – Fancy Office:

"I know dear. Yes, I know dear. Yes, understood." A very frazzled Bill Clinton looking toward a desk.

"He was the last obstacle to the white house. With him gone, life should get a lot easier." Hillary said, as her desk chair turned around to face Bill.

"Well, my job is done, so I am off to get a little relaxation."

"No whores today Bill. I have more work for you." Hillary starts typing away on a laptop computer.

"Oh come on honey. I have done much good work for you."

"My god Bill, you are even starting to sound like him." Hillary shook her head.

"Who? Kim Jong?"

"Yes, Kim Jong, you pantywaste."

And Hillary turned back to face Bill.

"Well, he is quite the endearing fellow you know. One day we were strolling through a park in Pyonggang..." Bill looked off in the distance as he reminisced.

"Bill...snap out of it, there are no parks in Pyonggang. In fact Bill, there is no grass in Pyonggang, or air to breathe, or food to eat. Now come on, let's get back to business. Have we killed the assassins that we sent to kill the assassins?"

"I think so. Somebody died, I know that." Bill starts dialing on his phone.

"Good. Crosscheck everything with Kim Jong so we can properly start the next phase of the plan." Hillary shows a wry smile.

"You got it dear. Anything else? Cucumber sandwich? Perrier?"

"You are such a pussy. Get the fuck out of here." Hillary waves at the door and Bill scuttles off.

3pm Sub Depot:

"What's the difference Josh?" Jeff did not seem to see the connection.

"The latest hit was not clean. It was dirty from the start fucker." Josh set his case down on the floor.

"So what, you think you'll get the drop on me? You think I do not come with backup? If you go against me you will have the whole company fighting against you. C'mon Josh, the work has been good! Let's not fuck things up." Jeff seemed intent on fixing things, as a few black SUVs entered the parking lot.

"That is backup? That is supposed to stop me from getting what I want?" Josh said, kicking his case on the back edge. "Ya know Jeff, when assassins get burned, it is all over, and the only thing to do is kill the enemy."

"There are a lot of groups around the world that could have done this Josh. And I guarantee you I had nothing to do with it. So let's stop this madness before things get out of control." Jeff stood up, with his hands up.

"Ya know what we specialize in Jeff?" Josh asked, looking out the window at the SUVs who now seemed to be unloading several well built men in dark suits.

"No, what do you specialise in Josh. Tell me."

"The right hit with the right escape plan." As he said that two automatic weapons popped out of his case and he began spreading fire at Jeff and the guys outside, who instantly started to return fire.

4pm The Oval Office:

"What is the problem Hillary?" the president asked, sitting behind his desk.

"I just want to be president so bad. I want to be president right now." Hillary said.

"Well, I have the job for now, but I am sure you will get in with the next election. Nothing to worry about I am sure." Obama stretched back in his chair.

"Barry, Bill says that all presidents kill people on the way to the white house. Is that true?"

"Of course. I killed dozens of people. I use some of the best assassins in the world. Do you need a reference?" Obama leaned forward.

"No, I think we have it covered. But I think recently maybe we have overstepped our bounds." Hillary looked at the floor.

"How is that?"

"Well, we had Kim Jong Il killed."

"What the fuck? You killed Kim? Oh well, I was almost there myself. I guess you saved the American taxpayer another assassin fee."

"Yeah, but the problem is the guy we used. He seems to be different than most of them.

You see, we have some intel that says he died in New Orleans the day before he killed Kim Jong in North Korea. So, of course we wonder how he could literally be in two places at once."

"Oh, that's no problem. Richard Pryor doubled for me at some campaign events several years ago."

"Richard Pryor? Isn't he dead?"

"Well, he was not in 2007."

"Got it. Hey, can I sit in your chair for a minute? Just to see what it feels like?" Hillary motioned to Barack's desk.

"Sure, enjoy." Barack got up and stood aside as Hillary sat down.

4pm North Korea:

"Oh...dear leader...I have failed you..." North Korean official laments.

"Sir...phone for you..."

"Cannot you see, idiot, me deep in sorry...dear leader..." more crying.

"It is the white house sir." the attendant speaks in perfect English.

"White house? Well, why didn't you say so....." suddenly the English is perfect. The attendant hands him the phone.

"Mr. Obama...yes...happy...uh..."

"What's going on sir?"

"Apparently President Obama is dead."

"What? Just now?"

"No, five minutes ago."

"Why is he calling us?"

"Apparently to warn of an assassin...."

"What are you going to tell him?"

"I cannot tell him anything." realizes he is still on the phone. "Yes sir, thank you for the warning."

"So since when do we get warnings from the white house for anything?" Suddenly a door opens. Kim Jong Il the father walks in.

"My God!" the attendants shout.

"I am back. I had to go away for a little while. But apparently my son could not handle the job so here I am."

The henchmen prostrate themselves.

5pm Plane to Washington:

"Something is not adding up." Shay says to mom.

"No shit. It looks like we might have a good ole Heinz 57 on our hands." Mom says.

"What is a Heinz 57?"

"Lots of red stuff, no real change in taste."

"So what is the plan from here?"

"Wait till Josh and Dad get back. We'll talk about it as a family." Josh and Dad return from the lavatory.

"Damn Southwest flights. Never enough toilet paper." Dad grumbled. Dad and Josh sat down.

"Well, guys, we have gotten ourselves into quite the predicament." Mom says.

"No kidding. I have not killed this many people in one day since I was 12." Josh says.

"So what is the next step?" Shay asks.

"You know what they say kid." Mom says. "All the shit in the USA flows to Washington DC."

"Of course. That is where my guns are made." Josh says. "They make the best Chinese knockoffs." Everyone laughs...then does kind of a double take.

"Well, that would be if the plane was actually on the way to Washington." And ominous voice was heard over the loudspeaker.

"The fuc..." Josh started to say.

"You see, kind Boudreaux's...you have meddled in our plans long enough..." suddenly the plane started to move and shake. The Boudreaux's gear up.

"You will never escape. We have chased you all day. This is the end for you." Suddenly Dad Boudreaux appears from the front of the plane. He pulls a gun and shoots the other Dad Boudreaux in the forehead.

"What the fuc..." Josh starts to say.

"He was an impostor. Those have been springing up all over the world. Various heads of state have been dying at the hands of me."

"Thank God...some plot..:" Mom says.

"Apparently an evil organization has been organizing World War III...but on a much higher scale than you might imagine...today Angela Merkel...David Cameron...and President Obama have all been killed. And of course Angola was raped first."

"Of course." Shay says.

"But I was able to break out of the prison they had me in in New Orleans in time to come get you guys. We have to jump off the plane. It is remote controlled and headed for a crash."

"How do you know all this? Mom asked.

"I am your husband dear. I know where you keep all your knives too." Mom Boudreaux blushes. "Parachutes guys...we are above Washington. Thankfully the villains who have booby trapped this plane are not good with Google Maps."

The Boudreauxs strap on parachutes and hop out of the plane.

12am Oval Office:

The Boudreaux's parachute directly into the oval office. Josh with guns drawn of course. No one is there except them.

"That was a hell of a long drop. It went from 5pm to 12am." Shay noticed.

"Cheap movie. No budget ya know." Dad says.

Suddenly Hilary Clinton strolls through the door, seemingly taken aback by the presence of the Boudreauxs.

"You are supposed to be dead!" she exclaims.

"Yeah, well so is your crusty vagina!" Josh screams, raising his gun.

"Hold off on that Josh." an ominous British accent is heard from the hallway.

"No way! Not another big name character." Shay complains.

"Oh come on Josh. You know I would be the best at all of this." Daniel Craig walks in.

"Of course! I always knew that. You are my hero!" Josh exclaimed.

"Unfortunately we are barely at page 50. We have to kick out another page or so of plot and action."

"So why all the dead leaders?" Mom asks.

"Well...who would run the world better than James Bond? He always knows what to do. He always gets laid. Always kills the bad guy. And he lives all the time, almost like Allah. Kinda like Jesus. But more like Allah..."

"So how do we end the movie?" Shay asks.

"Why don't we all just get in a fistfight that then escalates into a gunfight that then escalates into a nuclear war? Isn't that all Judd Apatow does now?"

Fistfight...gunfight...nuclear war.

Made in the USA
Las Vegas, NV
28 September 2024